MEDAL OF HONOR

Chris Ryan has fougl
around the globe.

He was the Commander of the Sniper squad
within the anti-terrorist team of the SAS.

He was the only member of an eight man patrol
on the Bravo Two Zero Gulf War mission in
Iraq who, when the mission was compromised,
fought his way to freedom.

His ordeal made history as the longest escape
and evasion by an SAS trooper, for which he
was awarded the Military Medal.

First published in Great Britain in 2010 by
Coronet, an imprint of Hodder & Stoughton.
An Hachette UK company

1

Copyright © Chris Ryan 2010

The right of Chris Ryan to be identified as
the Author of the Work has been asserted
by him in accordance with the Copyright,
Designs and Patents Act 1988.

A CIP catalogue record for this title is
available from the British Library.

ISBN 9781444707915

Typeset in Berthold Akzidenz Grotesk
Designed by Intercity
www.intercitystudio.com

Printed and bound in Spain by
Graficas Estella

Hodder & Stoughton policy is to use papers
that are natural, renewable and recyclable
products and made from wood grown
in sustainable forests. The logging and
manufacturing processes are expected to
conform to the environmental regulations of
the country of origin.

Hodder & Stoughton Ltd
338 Euston Road
London NW1 3BH

www.hodder.co.uk

CHRIS RYAN
MEDAL OF HONOR™

CORONET

ACKNOWLEDGEMENTS

With thanks to the teams at Electronic Arts and Mischief PR for this opportunity and to my agent Barbara Levy, publisher Mark Booth, Charlotte Haycock and the rest of the team at Coronet.

CONTENTS

FOREWORD

This all started with an introduction. It was a chance meeting with a unique group of individuals that would lead to the dramatic change in one of the most storied franchises in gaming history. For the first time in eleven years, Electronic Arts had decided to move Medal of Honor out of World War II and into the modern era and the fight in Afghanistan. The series has had a long tradition of telling the soldier's story in an honorable and respectful way, devoid of any politics or debate. However, this was a new war with a new enemy. And standing in front of us was a new type of warrior – The Tier 1 Operator.

We've all seen the movies, we've read the books and have been told larger-than-life stories of men who eat snakes, shoot with surgeon-like skill, and shit Kevlar. But where do these men come from? What makes them tick? Are these stories true, or are they myths? And most importantly, what do you say to a handful of these gentlemen, standing a few feet in front of you, in an effort to convince them it would be a good idea to tell the world their story and to do so in the form of a video game?

You don't say anything. You just listen.

You quickly learn it's not about them. It's not about the enemy. And, it's certainly not about the medal. It's about the man. It's about a community of warriors. It's about sacrifice and brotherhood. It's about commitment and purpose. A life-test. About the drive in an individual, so deep that when the world around them has gone to shit, their first thought is, "I can fix this" – with a reserved, quiet confidence. It's about the type of man who runs toward gunfire instead of away from it. The type of individual who thinks perfect isn't good enough, with great humility. It's about the truth. It's about respect. It's about honesty and integrity in one's beliefs and actions. It's about Honor.

Before us stood a group of men who had sacrificed their whole lives for the Honor of becoming what they are and the privilege of standing alongside men of equal character. They have been held in high regard, celebrated and written about in books and in movies – and now in Medal of Honor. It has been an amazing journey since that first fateful meeting. And in the end we have found our truth. And it has absolutely nothing to do with the fabled myths, folklore, or legends of dedicated men. Our truth is in our intent, and our intent is to simply say thank you. Thank you to the Operators around the world who keep our enemies frightened in their beds at night – so we may sleep peacefully in ours.

GREG GOODRICH
EXECUTIVE PRODUCER
MEDAL OF HONOR
JULY, 2010

GLOSSARY

BCR /
BATTLE CASUALTY
REPLACEMENT

BERGEN /
ARMY BACKPACK

CAFTAN /
A LOOSE ANKLE-LENGTH
GARMENT WITH LONG SLEEVES,
TRADITIONALLY WORN IN
ARAB COUNTRIES

CAM /
CAMOUFLAGE

CENTCOM /
UNITED STATES CENTRAL
COMMAND

DISHDASH /
A SHORTENING OF THE WORD
DISHDASHA. A DISHDASHA IS
RATHER LIKE A CAFTAN – IN THAT
IT'S AN ANKLE-LENGTH GARMENT
USUALLY WITH LONG SLEEVES,
WORN IN ARAB COUNTRIES.
CAN ALSO BE KNOWN AS A
THAWB OR THOBE, KANDURA,
KHAMEEZ, OR SURIYAH

FOB /
FORWARD OPERATIONS BASE

FRAG /
FRAGMENTATION GRENADE

FRIEND /
SPRING LOADED CAMMING
DEVICE (SLCD) USED IN ROCK
CLIMBING

IR FILTER /
INFA RED FILTER

LZ /
LANDING ZONE

M4 CARBINE /
RIFLE

MBITR /
RADIO

MRE /
MEAL, READY-TO-EAT

NV /
NIGHT VISION

OP /
OBSERVATION POST

RPG /
ROCKET PROPELLED GRENADE

SAS /
SPECIAL AIR SERVICE

SBS /
SPECIAL BOAT SERVICE

SHAMAG /
TRADITIONAL HEAD SCARF MADE
FROM A SQUARE OF CLOTH
(USUALLY COTTON) AND FOLDED
AND WRAPPED IN VARIOUS
STYLES AROUND THE HEAD

SIG P226 /
PISTOL

SITREP /
SITUATION REPORT

THE STAN /
AFGHANISTAN

UAV /
UNMANNED AERIAL VEHICLE

WADI /
ARABIC TERM REFERRING TO A
VALLEY OR A DRY RIVERBED

SO, YOU WANT TO KNOW WHAT HAPPENED THAT NIGHT?

It should have been nothing. Nothing for me, anyway. I'd been in The Stan since a few days after Bin Laden decided to play demolition derby with the Twin Towers. Hereford one day, Hindu fucking Kush the next. Almost lost track of how long I'd been out here. Two weeks? Three? The days and nights merged into one. Theatre like this, you just keep on keeping on. Those AQ and Taliban fucks don't care if they slot you the day you arrive or the day you leave, so you can't switch off until you're on an aircraft out of there.

Even so, I thought I'd seen my share of the action. The Regiment had its teams out on the ground that night, and so did the American Tier 1 units. That night they were called AFO Wolfpack and AFO Neptune. Their purpose: reconnaissance. The Taliban regime in Kabul was known to be harbouring Al-Qaeda groups. Bin Laden himself was probably nearby. We were there to locate these groups and, if necessary, eliminate them. It meant long stretches on the ground. Take it from me that the last couple of weeks had been intense.

I was on hand that night as battle casualty replacement, along with a handful of my US counterparts. Truth was, though, I expected to have one more night in this forward operating base and then, come sunrise, a transport home, for a little bit anyway, so I could brief my colleagues on what to expect out here. For now my kit was squared away and I was just looking forward to a few days away from the front line.

The FOB was basic. A plateau of flat earth surrounded on all sides by a ring of craggy mountains. It was hotter than two rats fucking in a wool sock. Give it a couple of months, though, and these peaks would be covered in snow. That was the problem with Afghanistan. Extremes. The people who lived here were used to it. It made them hard. Easy to underestimate, and that would be a mistake. The engineers had erected a couple of tents on the northern side of the FOB, which the Regiment and SBS lads shared with the Tier 1 boys. When we weren't out on the ground, these tents were where we took our briefings, ate and slept. *Tried* to sleep, I should say. Not easy with the constant comings and goings of old Russian helicopters. But hey, you get used to dog-tired being your default state.

The sun was setting over the mountains on that last evening. Pretty enough, if that's your scene. No wonder this region used to be part of the hippie trail. One look at it now, though, would be enough to make a hippie choke on his reefer. The FOB was dotted with troops either arriving or departing; choppers thundered up above us and disappeared over the brow of the mountains. The machinery of war everywhere. I was sitting on a metal flight case, my rifle by my side, tearing open an MRE and thanking God that I wouldn't have to eat too many more of these for a while, when a figure stood over me, blocking out the sunlight.

'*Jee*-sus, Jock.' A slow, Southern drawl. 'What in the name of *fuck* is that?'

I looked up. The guy standing two metres away from me had a beard as dark as his shades and a black and white shamag draped round his neck. Impossible to see his eyes, and I reckon Dusty liked it that way. The beard, and his brown, weathered skin, made him look more native than an Afghan carpet. That was why we all wore beards – to give us a chance of blending into the towns and villages.

'Dinner,' I told him, and I started scooping out the cold meatball and pasta stodge from inside its foil case. American MREs were in a different league to ours. No point bitching about it. Food was food. Fuel. Nothing more. I swallowed a mouthful and looked up again. He was still looking over me. 'What is this, Dusty – a sunset dinner for two?' Dusty shook his head. 'You Brits…' he started to say. He never finished, because just then another voice reached our ears – a thick Boston accent, curt and no-nonsense.

'Jock, Dusty, we're on. Briefing area, now.'

The voice belonged to Voodoo. He didn't look at us as he walked behind Dusty towards the tents. Not his style. Not ours to hang around either. When you're a battle casualty replacement, the word to stand by generally means there's a man down in the field. I wolfed down a couple more mouthfuls of food, then hurried with Dusty towards the briefing area of the nearest tent.

The briefing area was cordoned off from the rest of the tent by a line of plywood panels. Nowhere to sit. Just a board with a satellite map pinned to it, and a US Army Intelligence Officer who called himself Jackal, along with a couple of his guys I didn't recognize, standing by. He was one of those men with a permanent frown, and beads of sweat on his balding head. He looked impatient.

'Where the hell's Rabbit?' Jackal asked as we congregated around the map.

'Rabbit's right here.' I looked over my shoulder and there he was, stern-faced and narrow-eyed. Rabbit got his name on account of his six kids, but you never saw the ladies' man or the doting daddy out here. All you saw was the warrior.

Jackal nodded. 'OK, gentlemen. Listen up. First things first, breathe easy. This is *not* a BCR operation. We have no casualties.'

''Alle-fuckin'-luia,' said Dusty.

'So what's happening?' Voodoo demanded, chomping at the bit, as usual.

Jackal raised one eyebrow and looked at us: two Neptune, one Wolfpack, and one SAS. Unconventional to say the least. 'We need a team ready for immediate deployment. You're it.' He tapped at the map. 'This is the village of Pajay, thirty miles north-east of here.'

I looked at the map. Big village, small town. Take your pick. A mile east to west, about the same north to south. Mountain range on the northern edge, fuck all but desert to the south.

'Pajay is surrounded by run-down compounds and outbuildings, but these are mostly deserted and have been since the Russian occupation.

But the village itself has a fairly large population – somewhere in the high hundreds. It's also, to the best of our knowledge, littered with AQ. Seems we haven't done a good enough job of sweeping the assholes out of that area.'

'I'll get my broom,' Voodoo said.

Jackal ignored him. 'This,' he continued, holding up a grainy photograph, 'is your target. Name of Malouf. Fine figure of a man. Collects taxes for the local warlord, Mahmoud Afridi.'

We all studied the picture. Malouf was a jowly man with small, piggy eyes and a wispy beard. 'I shot better-looking razorbacks than him back home,' Dusty noted.

'Well, you won't be shooting this one. CENTCOM want the contents of this dude's head. All our intel suggests his boss is an enthusiastic partner of the Taliban.'

None of us looked surprised at that. It was no secret to anyone that the Americans were about to hit the Taliban hard and fast. The Afghan warlords had a choice to make: pave the way to work with the Americans, or continue to back the Taliban. Or, knowing the way these people approached things, do both. Some of the warlords were firmly in the Taliban's pockets, though, and it seemed like this Afridi was one of them.

'It appears Malouf sees things a little differently,' said Jackal. 'He knows his boss's days are numbered. If Afridi goes, there won't be any taxes for our man to collect. He can see his livelihood disappearing, so he's willing to sell us information.'

'Ain't nothing like loyalty,' Dusty murmured.

'Warms the heart, doesn't it?' said Jackal. 'But this piece of shit, Malouf, claims to know the whereabouts of a high-value AQ target called Al-Zaranj. If he's telling the truth, that makes him and his information valuable. It also makes his situation precarious. We need to get our hands on him right now. He's too scared to leave Pajay by himself in case Afridi gets suspicious, so that means we need to go to him. And we need to do it now before anyone starts getting cold feet.' Jackal looked at each of us in turn. 'At 22.00 hours you'll be inserted into the vicinity of Pajay. The Ops Centre at MacDill knows where Malouf's going to be tonight. They'll guide you in by satellite to his position. Once you've located him, you'll decide if he's on the level, then get whatever intel you can out of him. This is in and out, gentlemen. Nobody wants this to go noisy. We don't even want anybody to know you've been in there. Once we have a fix on Al-Zaranj's location, we'll have a separate unit go in and pick him up.' Jackal inclined his head. 'Or take him out. Questions?'

There were none. Just four grim faces, ready to do whatever needed to be done. As for me, it looked like my last evening in The Stan was going to be more exciting than I thought.

'All right then,' Jackal announced. 'You leave in three hours. Get your kit together. Now.'

22.14 HRS.

The four of us sat alongside each other in the belly of a Russian MI-8 transport helicopter. Three Yanks, one Brit. Not your average set-up. I'd never worked with these Tier 1 guys before, not out on the ground, so I hoped the reputation they had was well earned. Were they thinking the same about me? Of course they were. In our world, reputation is everything. Lose that and you're on the way out. I reckoned we all knew that over the next few hours we'd have the opportunity to show what we were made of. Jackal had said in and out. Experience taught us that things were rarely that simple.

The inside of the MI-8 was fucking horrible. Rickety, noisy, the air thick with the stench of fuel, and almost unbearably hot. But the ordinary people of Afghanistan were used to seeing these aircraft since the Russian occupation of the 1980s. The Tier 1 lads were using them to get around in an attempt to disguise who they were. Rabbit was next to me, twirling his lucky talisman a few inches in the air, then catching it and repeating the operation. The talisman in question was, of course, a rabbit's foot, and Rabbit kept it on him at all times. So far the charm had worked well, even though we all knew that out on the ground luck had little to do with anything.

Afghanistan was rapidly becoming the most dangerous theatre in the world. It was classified information that we were in the country, but the Taliban and their AQ buddies sure knew we were there. Every step we took out on the ground was a dangerous one.

In the built-up areas we risked being outnumbered at any moment. Even away from the villages and towns we were under the constant threat of long-range sniper fire or ambushes. Let your concentration drop for a second and you're going home in a box. Either that or you get a starring role in the next Al-Jazeera news bulletin. In circumstances like that, training, expertise and sheer bloody-mindedness to do the job well were more important than any lucky charm, and the guys with me in the MI-8 had those tools in spades.

We had other tools too. M4 carbines, locked and loaded, with replacement magazines of 5.56 rounds stashed in our ops waistcoats. These rounds were the hard-hitting 77-grain rather than the standard-issue 62-grain green tips. More violent fragmentation at short range meant the bad guys were less likely to stand up again once they'd been hit. My rifle was suppressed. It wouldn't totally silence it, but it meant that if we found ourselves in a contact in a built-up area, it would be more difficult for the enemy to locate me from the sound of my weapon. I had my Sig P226 strapped to the inside of my leg; the others had theirs wherever it was most comfortable: round the ankle or slung across the chest. Each of us had a satellite marker strapped to his arm, there to transmit our location back to MacDill Air Force Base in Florida, and night-vision goggles on our heads. Patrol comms were fitted – MBITR radios, with an earpiece in my right ear, and a small boom mike by my mouth; and, in each of our ops waistcoats, a pouch containing our Iridium sat phones – connected up to our earpiece and mike – for communications with MacDill. Our clothes were made of rough Afghan material – no sign of the military camo that would instantly mark us out as foreign troops. Each of us wore a kneepad on one knee, to protect the joint when we got down into the firing position. Our heavy caftans and shamags were musty and sweat-filled, but they were almost as important as our personal weapons. If you're heading into a hornets' nest, you need to look like a hornet. Otherwise you get stung.

At the other end of the chopper, by the tailgate, were our quad bikes – squat and khaki-coloured, with fat, sturdy tyres – each one fixed to the aircraft with a green cargo strap.

'Two minutes out!' The loadie's voice came over the noise of the chopper's engines. '*Two minutes out! Let's go, guys!*'

Voodoo looked at the rest of us and we nodded at him, just as the loadie started undoing the cargo straps. The MI-8 was already losing height when we took our places on the quad bikes, fixing our Bergens to the rack on the front, the back racks already being used to carry jerrycans of petrol. Cam nets were fixed to the vehicles, and by the side of the quad was a rifle mount. Fuck that. I preferred to have mine slung over my shoulder where I could get at it, and a quick glance around showed me that the others felt the same. I was the first to engage the red starting button on the right-hand side of the handlebars; the others quickly followed suit and we waited – with the quads already knocked into forward drive – for the chopper to touch down. None of the flight crew wanted to be on the ground for a second longer than was necessary, so we had to be ready to go.

There was a gentle bump as the MI-8 touched down. The tailgate immediately lowered to reveal nothing but a cloud of dust kicked up by the rotary blades, and a faint glow as the dust hit the blades and caused a spark. Voodoo was down, almost before the tailgate hit the ground, pulling off sharply to the right and vanishing into the dust cloud as Dusty followed, then me, then Rabbit. We were off the aircraft in less than ten seconds, and emerged through the brownout on to a featureless plain where the rumble of the MI-8 sounded even louder than usual. The four of us travelled about twenty metres from the chopper – far enough to be out of the range of the downdraught – before stopping.

I looked back over my shoulder to see the chopper, still surrounded by dust, its blades still sparking. Over the comms I heard Dusty's voice.

'So long, little bird.'

Right on cue the MI-8 started to rise. The dust settled and within ten seconds the aircraft was just a silhouette against the stars. The noise of its engines disappeared into the night, leaving us alone in the silence.

I took a moment to get my bearings. The MI-8 had inserted us fifteen miles due south-west of Pajay – far enough for the aircraft to land unnoticed by any AQ or Taliban in the village, close enough for us to approach by quad. There was a bright full moon, large but low enough in the sky for a quarter of it to be obscured by the peak of a mountain to the north. The ground was baked hard and stony, and twenty metres away I could see a long crack in the earth, about a metre wide and with a few spindly plants bravely trying to force their way skywards. I'd spent enough time on the ground to know that our path to Pajay would be full of these treacherous cracks and inlets. We'd have to go carefully.

Voodoo's voice over the comms. 'I'm getting on to base. Jock, join the call. Dusty, Rabbit, watch our backs.' Voodoo and I dialled in to our command centre at MacDill. 'Zero, this is Voodoo, Zero, this is Voodoo. Do you copy?'

A pause, then a crackle and a distant-sounding voice: 'Go ahead, Voodoo.'

'We're on the ground, the bird has flown.'

'Roger that. We have your position. Repeat, we have your position. Advance to target.'

'Check.'

We disconnected the call.

'Dusty, what's our bearing?'

Dusty pointed due northeast. Total confidence.

'You boys follow me,' he said.

'Roger that.'

We switched on our headlights. To the naked eye, no visible light emerged from the quads' headlamps as they'd been covered with IR filters; but as soon as we engaged our NV goggles, the beams illuminated the ground ahead of us for a good ten or fifteen metres, maybe more. I looked up. The Afghan night sky, impressive at any time, glowed like an acid trip through the NV. No time for stargazing, though. Dusty had already moved forward.

We drove slowly. No prizes for being first. At five miles per hour, the noise of the quads' engines was barely audible. It meant that as we approached, any reception party in Pajay could neither see us nor hear us until we were right on top of them.

There were other reasons to go slowly. The ground was treacherous – bumpy, stony and with sudden cracks that seemed to appear from nowhere, especially given that we only had the IR beams to light the way. And as we travelled, I tried not to think of the risk of legacy mines, left over from the Soviet invasion twenty years previously. The Russkies had mined the place to fuck, and half the things were still there. Just three days ago I'd had to pump a ten-year-old kid full of morphine after a mine had blasted his leg off. He was never going to survive more than a few minutes, but at least the drug made his final moments a little less agonizing.

We drove in silence, each man concentrating on the path ahead. Back at the FOB we could shoot the shit all day long, but now we'd only speak when necessary.

It took two or three hours before the low buildings of Pajay emerged from the distance. Our patrol stopped at the edge of a wide wadi. The dried-up riverbed was about ten metres across and two metres deep. We found a point on the bank where the incline was shallow enough to drive the quads down. The bottom of the wadi oozed with a thin film of mud – the remnants of the river. Give it a couple of months and it would be flowing with melted water from the snow-covered peaks, but for now it was wet enough to spatter our clothes as we drove around to find a suitable place to hide the bikes. It was Rabbit who found a section of the bank with an overhanging ledge and enough low brush to camouflage the gear. We got off the bikes, parked up, covered the gear with cam nets and regrouped.

'How far to the village?' Rabbit asked.

'I'll recce,' I said. I pulled my Kite night sight from my Bergen and, leaving the others by the quads, scrambled up to the northern edge of the wadi, keeping my head low. I pressed my body down into the earth and looked through the sight, focusing in on the nearest building I could make out. Difficult to tell what it was from this distance. It was tall, maybe twenty metres high, and looked like some kind of medieval watchtower. The scale on the sight told me it was 1700 metres away. I scanned left and right, pulling the focus in and out to search for any threats. Nothing. I could make out the outskirts of the village itself about fifty metres beyond the watchtower, and as I scanned west I could see what looked like a compound, but run-down and decrepit. I remembered what Jackal had said about Pajay being surrounded by tumbledown structures like that. Seemed like the intel was good. I rolled back down to the wadi bed.

'OK, fellas. A mile to go. There's what looks like an ancient lookout post ahead of us on the outskirts, but no lights in the vicinity. We can take cover there, then get base to guide us in.'

'Spot any gizzies in the vicinity?' Voodoo asked.

'Negative. Looks like everyone's sleeping soundly, fellas.'

'Yeah.' Dusty's expression was dark. 'Either that or they play a mean game of hide-and-seek.'

We approached in single file so we didn't present too wide a target for any shooters who did happen to be facing out from the watchtower, each man leaving about twenty metres between him and the guy ahead. I kept my rifle at the ready, the butt pressed in firmly to my right shoulder, ready to engage if need be. But there was no sight or sound of anyone as we grew near to Pajay; just the occasional howl of a dog barking in the darkness.

'I don't fucking like it,' said Dusty once we'd congregated by the watchtower. My first impression through the scope had been right – this thing looked like a relic from another century. It was old and neglected and part of the roof had fallen in. On the south wall was some kind of graffiti, but even that was faded. 'Where is everybody? *Nowhere's* this quiet.'

He was right. The place was like a morgue and Dusty wasn't the only one to have a bad feeling about this. Not bad enough to make us want to turn back, though. We were here to do a job, and we had no intention of leaving until the job was done.

Voodoo took control. 'The Taliban might have imposed a curfew,' he said. 'Last time I checked, they weren't too hot on big nights out. Means if we bump into anyone, it's probably a bad guy.' He pointed at the two corners on this side of the building. 'Rabbit, take the left, Dusty the right. Jock, let's get on to base. The sooner they can guide us to this Malouf dude, the sooner we can get the hell out of here.'

Sounded like a plan to me. We used our sat phones to dial in. 'Zero, this is Voodoo. Do you copy?'

A pause.

'Voodoo, this is Zero. How you guys doing out there?'

'We're ready for the walkthrough.'

'Roger that.' A pause. 'There's a wide street due north of your position. Advance 175 metres to a crossroads. This is the junction with the main market street of Pajay, so expect hostiles. Repeat, expect hostiles.'

Voodoo pointed at me and Rabbit. 'Take the lead,' he instructed.

We knew what to do without talking about it. While Voodoo and Dusty covered us from behind, Rabbit and I moved forward, round the side of the watchtower. I could see the wide street up ahead, about fifty metres away, but between here and there was a patch of open ground with only two small mulberry trees to break it up. I jabbed my finger towards the trees, Rabbit nodded and together we ran towards them. Once we were there, we took cover. Rabbit pointed his rifle towards the street; I pointed mine back the way we'd come. '*Go!*' I hissed over the radio, and seconds later I saw the silhouettes of Dusty and Voodoo running towards us. They didn't stop at the mulberry trees, but continued running past while Rabbit and I gave them cover, only stopping by the entrance to the wide street. They took up position, one on either corner.

'*Go!*' came Voodoo's voice in my earpiece, and Rabbit and I moved on.

We continued this leapfrogging movement up towards the crossroads. From what I could make out of Pajay, the place was a shithole. Half the houses – if that's what you wanted to call these run-down collections of breezeblocks, rotten timbers and corrugated iron – were clearly deserted. Some of them didn't even have front doors. From the occasional house we saw a glow emanating from behind shuttered windows. But not a single person. Until. . .

'Tango straight ahead,' I reported.

Rabbit and I were approaching the crossroads when, about twenty metres away, a figure walked from the left into our line of sight. We pressed ourselves into the shadow of a doorway, hoping that whoever it was would wander off in the opposite direction. No such luck. The figure sauntered towards us. He had a cigarette in his mouth, and as he walked past I saw a Kalashnikov slung over his right arm. Whoever this was, he wasn't just out for a midnight stroll.

He stopped, took a deep drag on his cigarette, the tip glowing briefly in the night, then walked past us. Ten metres from our position, about halfway between us and the others, he stopped again. He had the demeanour of somebody who was on guard, and while he stood in the middle of the street, we weren't going anywhere.

Voodoo's voice over the comms, not much more than a whisper. 'I'll talk to him. Any funny business, you know what to do.'

Rabbit got the guy in his sights while I loosened my knife. I found myself holding my breath as Voodoo stepped out from his hiding place into the street, his weapon slung across his back so that our man couldn't easily see it.

'*Salaam*,' he called. Voodoo might have been Southside Boston born and bred, but he had enough Pashto to converse with the locals. Mine was only just good enough to understand what they were saying. 'You got a cigarette, my friend?' he asked, sounding to my ear like a native.

I only got the gist of the man's unfriendly reply. 'What are you doing out on the street? There's a curfew... punishment...'

'Hey, friend, take it easy.' Voodoo spread his arms wide, displaying his palms to show how harmless he was. It didn't wash with our man. He started moving his AK round to his front.

That was my cue to move.

Rabbit could slot the guy in a second, but even a suppressed round would create more noise than we wanted to make. I covered the ten metres between me and the target as quietly as possible and in less than the time it took him to get his rifle in anything near a firing position. I was two metres behind him when he realized Voodoo wasn't his only problem, but by that time it was too late. I got my left hand over his mouth, my right knee into the small of his back and my blade against his neck.

One slice and he was down, unable to make any kind of noise as he died, because his larynx had been severed.

The fucker bled like a pig, but I ignored that. Our main problem was that a dead Taliban in the middle of the road would alert people to our presence if anybody found him. We needed to get him out of the way. Voodoo took his legs, I took his arms, and we moved him to the side of the road. We selected a house that looked deserted and hid the body just inside the doorway. Not exactly a great hiding place, and it wouldn't take long before the body started to stink. But by then we'd be long gone, and I couldn't help but think the villagers would scarcely mourn the death of a Taliban guard.

I was wiping my bloodied knife on the dead man's clothes when I heard a voice over the sat phone. 'Voodoo, this is Zero. You've stopped. Everything OK?'

'Everything cool,' Voodoo replied. 'Everything just cool.'

The control centre at MacDill continued to guide us in. We took a left at the crossroads, continuing in our leapfrog formation past the rickety, boarded-up stalls that lined the main road through Pajay. A few old motorbikes were propped up against some of the buildings, and the air smelt of spilled fuel, rotting garbage and animal shit. MacDill instructed us to make a right about fifty metres along the road, then directed us through a maze-like network of stinking side streets until we came to a single-storey dwelling that was slightly less of a dump than all the others. The roof was made of corrugated iron; the render on the blockwork was crumbling; but the door and windows looked a little sturdier, and the building was slightly larger than most. Yellow light seeped out from under the doorway.

'Voodoo, this is Zero. You are on target. Repeat, you are on target.'

'Roger that, Zero. We're going in.' Voodoo and I disconnected our sat phones. 'Dusty,' Voodoo said, 'Rabbit, watch the street. Jock, cover me.'

Dusty and Rabbit moved with barely a sound. Dusty hid in the shadow of a small alleyway about ten metres to the left of the building, got down on one knee in the firing position and aimed his rifle one way down the street. Rabbit took cover behind a pile of bald tyres just opposite him and pointed his weapon the other way. I took a few steps back from the building and covered the entrance while Voodoo, his M4 pressed hard into his shoulder, gave two light kicks on the door before stepping back five paces and waiting.

Nothing happened. All I could hear was my own breath.

Dusty over the headset: 'What's going on?'

'Fingers on triggers, Jock?' Voodoo breathed.

'Fingers on triggers.'

He kicked the door again, before stepping back once more.

Five seconds passed. Suddenly a shadow covered the yellow glow escaping from under the door. I pressed my finger a little more firmly against the trigger of my rifle.

The door opened slowly.

I narrowed my eyes as they adjusted to the sudden outpouring of light.

A figure was framed in the doorway, but it was not Malouf. This was an old woman, her back hunched, and her body swathed in black robes. She peered blindly out of the house, just as Voodoo approached with his weapon pointed directly at her. Whoever she was, she was a tough old bird. She glanced down at the barrel of Voodoo's carbine like she was looking at a troublesome child.

'Where is he?' Voodoo demanded in Pashto.

The old woman didn't speak. She just looked over her shoulder and stepped back into the room.

'Dusty, Rabbit, stay where you are. Jock, you're with me.'

We entered quickly. Voodoo took the area to the right of the door. I took the left. We were in a room about five metres square. On the floor there was an old, patterned Afghan carpet and the walls were bare apart from a single picture that showed a passage – probably from the Qur'an – in Arabic. Against one wall was an old wooden table with a decrepit lamp and a bare bulb. Sitting at the table was a fat, sweaty man – Malouf. His piggy eyes were full of fright and he shrank back when he saw us, but we ignored him for the moment. I covered that main room while Voodoo passed through the only other door, just by the table, to check the rest of the building. It took about twenty seconds before he returned. 'Clear,' he said.

I closed the main door, knowing that Dusty and Rabbit would cover our backs from outside. Only then did we lower our weapons and turn our attention to Malouf.

His eyes darted between us. 'I thought you would be here sooner,' he said in thickly accented English.

'Did you have somewhere else to be?' Voodoo asked, his voice dripping with sarcasm.

Malouf shook his head nervously. Sweat poured from his face. The old lady stood behind us in the corner of the room, her head bowed. She was saying something underneath her breath, but it was impossible to tell what. Voodoo jerked his thumb at her. 'She speak English?'

Malouf shook his head. 'No. Only me. Since a child I…'

'OK, Malouf,' Voodoo butted in. 'Let's hear what you've got to say.'

Malouf licked his fat lips. 'You want Al-Zaranj? I know where he is.'

'Oh yeah? Why should we believe you?'

Malouf's lip curled. 'You do not know what it is like to live here,' he said.

'From what I heard,' I interrupted, 'it sounds like you and your man Afridi do pretty well out of it.'

A flicker of annoyance crossed Malouf's face. 'I do what I need to make a living for my family. If it hadn't been me, Afridi would have found someone else. It does not mean I love the Taliban, or their Al-Qaeda friends.'

Malouf looked over at the old lady and issued a harsh instruction in Pashto. She shook her head and shrank into the corner, but then Malouf gave her a dangerous stare and she stepped towards us. Slowly she pulled her black robe off her shoulder.

Her body was thin and bony, but it wasn't this that caught our attention. It was the deep red scars that ran through her skin.

'My mother,' Malouf said. 'The Taliban beat her for walking outside with her head uncovered. The wounds became infected and she nearly died. You think that makes me glad? You think I want the Taliban to remain? This Al-Zaranj, if he and his Al-Qaeda associates are not driven from my country, it will only make the Taliban stronger and crueller. Everybody knows that. But you Americans, you can change all this.'

Malouf sat back. He looked exhausted from his little speech and his skin was sweatier than ever. Voodoo and I exchanged a look, then turned back to our informant.

'All right, Malouf,' said Voodoo. 'Let's have it. Where's Al-Zaranj?'

Malouf's piggy eyes narrowed. 'You have money for me?'

I felt myself sneering. 'So much for his morals.'

Voodoo shrugged. 'Money talks, bullshit walks,' he said. 'And that's true in Boston *and* Bagram.' He pulled out a wad of American dollars from his ops waistcoat and slapped them on the table. For a fat man, Malouf moved pretty fast, grabbing the notes like a greedy kid snatching the last cake and secreting them somewhere inside his grubby dishdash. Somehow his greed made me feel a bit better about the whole thing. Now we knew he was grassing up Al-Zaranj for money it all seemed a bit more on the level.

'OK, friend. You'd better start talking,' Voodoo told him. 'Where is he?'

'Here,' Malouf said. He suddenly looked very pleased with himself.

Voodoo and I shared another look. 'What do you mean, here?' I asked.

'Here in Pajay. Tonight. I can tell you where.'

This wasn't what we were expecting. Intel had never suggested Al-Zaranj was in Pajay itself. Our mission was to find Al-Zaranj's position, then extract immediately. If he *was* here, though, there wasn't a man among us who wouldn't want to go after him. All of a sudden, the whole nature of the operation had changed.

'Dusty, Rabbit, you getting this?' Voodoo spoke into his radio.

'Roger that,' came Dusty's voice. 'I say we smoke the fucker out.'

'Rabbit?'

'Count me in.'

'Jock?'

I wasn't so sure. I stepped up to Malouf – close enough to smell his sweat and his breath – then kneeled down and looked him straight in the eye. Malouf returned my look with a stony stare of his own. 'If you're shitting us,' I whispered to him, 'you'll be planting the old lady before dawn. That's the way you do things out here, isn't it?'

Malouf glanced over my shoulder to where his mother had retreated back into the corner.

'I swear,' he whispered hoarsely. 'I am telling you the truth.'

I stood up and turned back to Voodoo. 'He comes with us,' I said. 'If we're going after Al-Zaranj now, I want to know where this piece of shit is at all times.'

Malouf shook his head. 'No,' he stammered. 'If the Taliban see me out after curfew, I will be punished. My *mother* will be punished.'

I ignored him. 'I mean it, Voodoo. Leave him here and fuck knows who he'll send after us.'

Malouf was wringing his hands. 'I beg of you, do not make me leave. If they suspect me...'

Voodoo gave it a few seconds' thought. 'You're right,' he said after a moment. He narrowed his eyes. 'Malouf, you're coming with us.'

01.30 HRS.

We'd put the call through to MacDill, explaining what was going down and requesting official permission to go after Al-Zaranj. Two minutes later the word had come back. 'You're the guys on the ground. It's your call.'

We all needed to hear Malouf's instructions from the horse's mouth, so Dusty and Rabbit had joined us in the house. 'Al-Zaranj is in a compound on the northern outskirts of the village,' Malouf explained. His eyes were a little wild and he couldn't avert his gaze from our weapons.

'I thought all the compounds outside the village were clapped out,' I butted in.

'Clapped out?'

'Destroyed.'

'Most of them are,' Malouf agreed. 'But not this one.'

'Describe it.'

'It is large. Maybe thirty metres by thirty. But only one entrance. There are guards there – two of them, Al Zaranj's people. Inside the compound, I do not know how many. But not a lot, I think. Al-Zaranj came down from the mountains yesterday. He had only a few men with him.'

'What's the approach like?'

'Mountain slopes at the back, fields on the other three sides. Poppies. At this time of the year, very low. Maybe this high.' He lowered his hand to indicate a height of about half a metre.

'High enough to crawl through,' Voodoo

observed. 'What else, Malouf?'

The fat man shrugged. 'Nothing,' he said. 'It is all outside the village.' Then he inclined his head. 'Wait. There is a farm building on the other side of the field, opposite the front of the compound. But it is crumbling, like most of the other places. There will be no one there.'

'We can take your word for that, huh?' Dusty said under his breath.

Voodoo turned to me. 'Guards on the door.' He jerked his thumb in Malouf's direction. 'If we're going to have to fight our way in, we can't have him with us.'

Dusty narrowed his eyes. 'Damn right. I ain't clearing a compound with him draggin' ass behind us.'

Malouf was nodding. 'You are right – it is better I stay here. If they see I am gone, they might know something is wrong.'

Voodoo sniffed. 'Shut up, Malouf. We ain't leaving you anywhere. Dusty, you and me can head north; Jock, Rabbit, you take Malouf back to the quads. We'll take out this Al-Zaranj fuck, then RV with you back there.'

Voodoo turned to Rabbit and me. 'You good with that?'

'Check,' we said in unison. It wasn't that we didn't want to go after Al-Zaranj ourselves, but we knew the security of the unit was the most important thing. I stepped over to where Malouf was sitting and pulled him up by the scruff of his dishdash. 'OK, sunshine,' I told him. 'Let's boogie.'

We couldn't take the old woman with us – she'd just slow us down. But I wanted to leave her with something to think about. 'Malouf, tell your mother that if anyone comes after us, you'll be first person we kill.'

'Please let me stay…'

I put my gun to his head. 'Just do it.'

Malouf's eyes widened, but he murmured something to his mother, who stared at me like I was a monster. I gave her a fierce look back to make her believe I meant it.

'All right, Malouf,' Voodoo cut in. 'When we get outside, you do exactly what we say. Don't make any of us nervous. You start going off-piste and we'll shoot you off the slope.'

Malouf looked confused. 'What is off-piste?' he asked.

'Just do as you're told, OK?

He gulped nervously.

It was still eerily quiet outside the house. Even the dog that had been barking during our approach had grown silent. The moon was higher now and cast shadows on the stony ground of the village. Voodoo and Dusty melted away along the darker side of the street, heading the opposite way to that from which we'd arrived. I nodded at Rabbit, who hurried to the other corner of the street before waiting for us to leapfrog him.

Nudging Malouf between his podgy shoulder blades with the barrel of my rifle, I told him, 'Walk.'

'What if we see someone?' he hissed.

'You'd better hope we don't.'

I walked five metres behind him, weapon at the ready, looking around me for any unexpected movement. There was none. Pajay was as dead as a spent case. It took us ten minutes to get back to the deserted watchtower on the outskirts, and another twenty to force the stumbling and scared Malouf back to the wadi, where the quads were waiting for us, untouched. Twice he begged me to let him go back home. Twice I forced him on.

Just as Rabbit was forcing Malouf down on to his knees so he could keep guard over him, the radio crackled into life.

'Jock, Rabbit, this is Voodoo. We've located the compound. Repeat, we have located the compound.'

'Copy that,' I replied. 'Everything like Malouf described it?'

From the corner of my eye I saw Malouf nodding his head as Voodoo said, 'Bang on. We've checked inside the farm building. Empty. We're on the edge of the field, low down. Compound gate fifty metres from our position, over open ground.'

'You got company?'

'Just like the man said. Two gizzies, leaning on their fucking rifles. We're going in now.'

'It is how I described?' Malouf asked. 'You let me go home now. . .' One look silenced him.

I didn't like not being there with Voodoo and Dusty, and from Rabbit's face I could tell he didn't either. Doesn't matter who you are – any sprint across open ground is dangerous. Sure, they could take care of themselves, but four guys were better than two, no matter what the operational scenario.

Nothing we could do about it, though. We just had to wait and listen in.

Sixty seconds later there was a low thud over the radio, followed by a second. Suppressed gunfire. 'Guards down,' I said to Rabbit. He nodded, and I felt Malouf's eyes on me, hungry for more information about what was going on.

We waited in silence. A shuffling sound in my earpiece – Voodoo and Dusty covering the open ground, then another couple of suppressed thuds as they blasted their way into the compound.

'We're in.' Voodoo's voice was low and tense.

'What is happening?' Malouf asked.

'Shut the fuck up,' I told him. 'When you need to know something, I'll tell you.'

Malouf gave me a sour look and kept his gaze on me. I noticed his hand trembling. Good job we hadn't taken him with us. If he was all shitted up just listening, what would he be like close to the action?

The next two minutes felt like two hours. The silence on the radio was broken only by the occasional crash of a door being knocked in. No voices. No gunfire.

'*What is happening?*' Malouf asked again.

I didn't reply this time. I just gave him a look at the barrel of my weapon.

Finally I heard Voodoo's voice. 'Compound clear. It's fucking empty.'

'What do you mean?'

'How many ways do you want me to say it, Jock? Malouf's full of shit. There's no one here.'

I bore down on the sweating Afghan. He could obviously tell something was wrong, and there was fear in his eyes.

'What is it? What is wrong?'

'There's no one there, Malouf. The compound's empty.'

He looked genuinely astonished and started shaking his head. 'No,' he said. 'No, it is *not* empty. I *swear* it is not empty.'

I had to make a call in the heat of the moment. Did I believe him or not? Either he was a fucking good actor, or he was telling the truth.

'Malouf says there's someone there. He looks kind of convinced.'

'You know what I'm thinking?' Dusty's voice came over the radio. 'I'm thinking you don't put two armed guards outside a compound with nothing to guard. There's something else going on here.'

Dusty was right. This didn't add up. 'I say you exfiltrate,' I told them. 'Get the hell out of there. We can come in mob-handed, deal with it then.'

But Voodoo and Dusty weren't the exfiltrating types. It was what made them what they were.

'We're going to check again,' Voodoo said. 'If we don't find nothing on the second sweep, we'll bug out.'

'Roger that.'

Another silence. A minute. Maybe two. And then...

'We got something,' Voodoo breathed. 'A door behind a carpet on the wall. Missed it first time round.'

Rabbit and I exchanged a glance. 'I don't like it,' I murmured. I turned to Malouf. 'If you've got anything else to tell us, now's the time.'

Malouf shook his head. 'All I know is Al-Zaranj is there,' he said.

Silence again. Then the sudden, violent sound of a door splintering. I could picture Voodoo and Dusty entering this room, most likely with their NV on and IR beams from their weapons cutting through the darkness like lasers. I tensed myself for the sound of gunfire. None came. Just Voodoo's voice, slightly breathless.

'We've got a guy in here,' he reported. 'Strapped to a chair, looks unconscious. Jeez, whoever got to him did him over pretty bad.'

'What the hell do you mean, strapped to a chair?' I asked. 'That can't be Al-Zaranj.'

It was as I spoke these words that I saw it. It wasn't much, just the ghost of an expression on Malouf's face. A tightening round the eyes. A thinning of those podgy lips. He looked around, as if getting ready to run. . .

He was expecting something to happen.

'*Get out!*' I yelled into the comms. '*It's a trap! GET OUT!*'

Everything happened so quickly. The moment I shouted into my radio mike, I heard another noise over the headset: the faint ringing of a mobile phone in the compound. My heart was in my throat. We knew only too well how easily a mobile could be used to detonate an explosive device. Simply a matter of dialling the number.

A millisecond after the phone rang, I heard Dusty's voice. '*GET DOWN!*'

And then came the explosion.

I heard it through the headset first: a burst of white noise that almost deafened me. A second later the sound waves reached us: a low thud travelling across the desert and into the wadi.

Rabbit shouted, 'Dusty! Voodoo!'

Silence.

'*Dusty! Voodoo! Come in!*'

Still nothing. Rabbit and I looked at each other. We both knew this operation was rapidly going to shit before our eyes.

02.05 HRS.

When stuff goes wrong in the field, the important thing is to keep your head. Start to panic and you make mistakes, and we sure as hell couldn't afford any more of those.

Rabbit continued trying to raise Voodoo and Dusty. I turned my attention to Malouf. He'd got up to his feet and was backing away from me, looking like he might run. So I strode towards him and knocked him back down to the ground. I pulled my Sig from its holster and pressed it into his jowly neck. 'What the hell's going on?' I hissed.

The guy looked like he might piss himself with fear. 'He made me do it,' he rasped. 'He *made* me do it.'

'Who?'

'Afridi. He discovered that I was talking to the Americans. He took my daughter. He said he would...' Malouf looked away, as though ashamed. 'He said he would have her raped by all his men, then killed. Only if I did what he told me when you arrived would he free her.'

I had to breathe deeply for a moment to stop myself being consumed with rage. *Damn it*. Malouf had told us what we wanted to hear and we'd fucking fallen for it. We'd been played, and as a result, Voodoo and Dusty were... well, God alone knew what kind of state they were in.

I took Malouf by the throat. 'If my friends are dead,' I whispered, 'your daughter gets orphaned tonight.'

Malouf's eyes went wild. In another part of my brain I could hear Rabbit's urgent calls: '*Voodoo! Dusty! Do you copy?*'

I tried to focus on the job in hand. Was Malouf telling the truth? Impossible to say, and we didn't have time to fuck around with him. Dusty and Voodoo needed our help – now.

'Do you really know where Al-Zaranj is?' I hissed. 'Or have you been fucking with us all along?'

At first Malouf didn't answer, so I squeezed his throat harder. 'I mean it, Malouf. I'll fucking kill you here and now.'

'*Voodoo! Dusty! Come in...*'

'Please,' Malouf begged in strangled tones through the confusion. '*My daughter... my mother... please...*'

'Where's Al-Zaranj?'

'In the mountains.' He pointed vaguely back towards the village. 'There is a...' – he struggled to find the English word – 'a *valley*. North of here. It is called Bakharov. A stream runs through it, and there are caves. Al-Zaranj and his people are there. Afridi sends him food. The Taliban tell him to. They have been hiding for many weeks...'

I pushed him back down to the ground in disgust, and turned my back on him as he huddled up into a pathetic, frightened little ball. I hurried over to where Rabbit was crouched down, one finger to his earpiece. He gave me a severe look and shook his head. 'Either the comms are out or they're...'

He didn't finish the sentence, because suddenly our earpieces burst into a mess of radio static. Through it we heard the sound of coughing, and then. . .

'Jesus!' Voodoo's voice. 'I'm getting too old for this shit!'

'Christ's sake, Voodoo, I thought you were fried. What's your status?'

'The fucker was booby-trapped. Remind me to have a little word with Malouf next time I see him!'

'I already did. Is Dusty all right?'

'Roger that,' said Dusty.

'I heard a phone detonating the device,' I told them. 'It means they know you're there!'

'Fine,' Voodoo replied. 'Let 'em come. Me and Dusty are ready for them!'

'Don't leave the building, guys. If the Taliban have eyes on, they'll slot you the second you step outside. I'll be there with Rabbit as quick as we can!'

I turned to Rabbit. 'Get the quads ready,' I told him. 'We need to double it over there. I'll deal with Malouf!'

Our informant was still hugging the ground. I pulled him up. 'Let's go, shit-for-brains. We're getting out of the wadi!'

'Where are we going?'

'MOVE!'

Malouf stumbled up the southern bank with me right behind.

'Get on your knees,' I ordered him.

He gave me an appalled look, then shook his head. 'No,' he begged. 'Not that. Please. . .'

'*Get on your knees!*'

I pushed down on his shoulders and he flopped to the ground, his head bowed. The fucker clearly thought I was going to do him there and then. I let him think that for a moment while I pulled two sets of plasticuffs from out of my waistcoat. I quickly tied his hands behind his back, then bound his ankles. Trussed up like that he wasn't going anywhere fast. He tried to say something, but didn't get more than a couple of words out before I stuffed his mouth with an oily rag that I used for cleaning my weapon.

'Lie down,' I said, and to help him along I pressed my knee into his back. He fell to his front. 'Stay like that if you want to live.'

Malouf tried to say something, but all that came out were a few muffled grunts. I took a piece of rope and attached one end to Malouf's legs, the other around a boulder on the edge of the wadi, then I reached into my Bergen and pulled out a Firefly which I clipped to the back of his clothes. A flick of its switch and the little device started transmitting a flashing infrared beam, which would be visible to NV-enabled air crews for miles around. Someone else could take Malouf off our hands. Rabbit and I had things to do.

As I scurried back down into the wadi, I called base on the sat phone. 'Zero this is Jock.'

'*Go ahead, Jock.*'

I gave them a quick sitrep, briefly filling them in on what had happened to Dusty and Voodoo. 'Malouf's got a Firefly,' I told them. 'If you want him, come and get him. Me and Rabbit are going after the others.' I didn't request permission, and they didn't offer it. Everyone knew that if our brothers were in trouble, our only thought was for getting them out. Less than a minute later Rabbit and I were on the quads, speeding along the wadi until we found a place on the north side where we could exit. Then we headed towards the village.

Our way was lit by the IR beams, but we couldn't afford the luxury of going slowly to keep down the noise of the engines. We skirted round the western edge of the village, past a number of the ramshackle compounds on the outskirts that Jackal had mentioned during our briefing. We stopped behind a little group of outbuildings almost precisely due west of the village, about 200 metres out.

As soon as the quads came to a halt, Rabbit and I took cover behind them and hunkered down into the firing position. These outbuildings *looked* deserted, but that didn't mean they were, so we needed to be ready for any incoming fire.

We stayed like that for sixty seconds. Nothing. I lowered my gun, took out my Kite sight and edged round to the side of the outbuildings. From here I could use the scope to see across open ground to the northern edge of the village. After thirty seconds I'd focused in on what looked like the compound Malouf had described. There was a wall right along the front, about three metres high and fifteen metres long. The rectangular entrance door was bang in the middle, and if I looked carefully I could still see the remnants of a cloud of dust from the blast settling on it – a visual echo of what had gone on fifteen minutes before. There were also figures moving around the open ground in front of the compound. I counted them carefully. There appeared to be five.

A crackle over my earpiece, then Voodoo's voice. He sounded tense. Couldn't blame him. 'Where the hell are you guys?'

'If your compound is twelve o'clock, we're at nine o'clock,' I told him. 'I've got you on my scope. I've counted five tangos in your vicinity, but they're moving around, so there could be more. I reckon they're too scared to enter the compound in case you're still alive.'

'Damn right. You see the barn on the other side of the field to our south?'

I scoped it out. 'Roger that.'

'If anyone has eyes on us, that's where they'll be,' Voodoo said. 'You need to check that building for snipers before laying into the others. Try the roof.'

Voodoo was right, as usual. 'Sit tight,' I told him. 'We'll deal with it.'

I edged backwards towards where Rabbit was waiting for me. 'We'll head north by foot,' I told him. 'Can't risk the noise of the quads. There's another old building fifty metres to the west of Voodoo and Dusty. It's on slightly higher ground – we should be able to use it as a firing point.'

Rabbit nodded. 'We got to keep this quiet, Jock,' he said. 'If it starts to go noisy, they'll be coming at us from all sides.'

We set off using our standard leapfrog formation – one of us in the firing position while the other covered ground as quickly and as silently as possible – and reached our potential firing location within five minutes. At some point in the past this building, whatever it was, had been hit from above by a bomb big enough to destroy the whole thing. The remnants of a square outer wall were still vaguely intact in places, but most of it was tumbledown and demolished, with weeds growing up through the rubble. Hunks of rusted metal were littered around the interior, all that was left of old vehicles that had been corroded and crushed by the extremes of the Afghan climate. However, this flattened wreck of a building suited our purposes just fine. We managed to attain a bit of height by climbing up on to a pile of rubble that was once part of the wall facing towards the village. Then we lay on our fronts, facing southeast towards the barn.

Even with the naked eye we could see the figures moving about the open ground in front of the compound. Impossible to tell what they were doing there – waiting for reinforcements, most likely, before they stormed the compound to check their booby-trap had done its work. If that was their plan, it meant we had to work quickly.

These enemy weren't our biggest problem. Out in the open like that, we could nail them in a few seconds. I was more concerned about any hidden shooters. They had to be our priority.

I got out the Kite again and trained it on the flat roof of the barn. Ten seconds to focus in, then I saw them. There were two guys, one at each corner of the roof, which made them about ten metres apart. They were lying perfectly still on their fronts, with their rifles trained on the front door of the compound.

'Two tangos on the roof of the barn,' I told Rabbit. 'You shoot, I scope.' We were both good enough snipers to take either role.

Rabbit didn't answer. He just got right down to preparing his weapon while I used the Kite to scan the area for evidence of wind movement. But it was a still night. The few trees I could see in the distance were motionless, and there was no evidence of dust movement on the ground.

'Wind movement zero,' I said quietly. 'No need to adjust the shot.' Sweat dripped from my forehead and into my eyes.

By now Rabbit had his weapon prepped and was looking through the sights.

'We have two targets,' I repeated. 'You got them?'

'I got 'em.'

'Distance to nearest target, 480 metres.' Just within the range of the M4, but not an easy shot to make. 'Distance to second target, 487 metres. Take the closest target first.'

A pause.

'No room for fuck-ups, Rabbit,' I said. 'We want these two down without the guys on the ground knowing what's happening. Take your time, buddy. Let's make each shot a kill.'

Rabbit's breathing went very slow.

Ten seconds passed.

Twenty. I kept my eye on the target in the Kite. And then. . .

'Take the shot,' I said.

'Taking shot now.'

Rabbit squeezed the trigger. There was a low thump from the weapon and I could sense him controlling the recoil. I kept my eye on the target and saw the sniper's body immediately judder. A direct hit.

'First target down,' I confirmed.

The second sniper looked round. All he could have heard was the sound of the round entering his comrade's body, but that had been enough to alert him to something being wrong. Rabbit was on to him before he could do a thing about it.

'Taking shot now,' he said.

Another low thump from the suppressed M4. I clearly saw the round hit the second target in the head.

'Second target down.'

We didn't move. The worst mistake you can make after firing a sniper round is to assume the job's finished. I scanned over to the open ground between the barn and the compound. There were still only five enemy there, and they clearly hadn't noticed that the two snipers had been taken out. I continued to pan left and right, keeping my eyes peeled for any sign of unexpected enemy movement. But there was none.

'Job's a good 'un,' I said. 'Now let's take the rest of these fuckers and get the hell out of here.'

02.50 HRS.

The four of us consulted over the radio.

'Snipers down,' I reported. 'We still have five tangos in front of the compound. No sign that they know their men are down. My guess is they're still waiting for reinforcements before going in.'

Voodoo's voice was brisk. 'How far away are you?'

'Five hundred metres.'

'How close can you get without them seeing you?'

I gave it a moment's thought. It was open ground between us and them, and the moon was bright. Hardly fucking ideal – but with Voodoo and Dusty needing support, there was no way we were going to stay hidden behind this mound of rubble. 'I reckon we can get to within 250 metres. Closer than that, it might go noisy.'

'It's gonna go noisy any which way, my friend. We'll give you three minutes to approach – then we'll get a couple of frags over the wall and bug out. You guys do the mopping up for us, huh?'

'You got it.'

Rabbit and I clambered down from the rubble and switched our M4s to fully auto. We were advancing to contact, and in a situation like this there'd be no time for precision shooting. We tabbed forwards, separated by a distance of about ten metres, our rifles pressed firmly into our shoulders and pointed squarely in the direction of the enemy.

Silence all around. Just the noise of our footsteps crunching on the stony ground.

A minute passed. Two.

'That's close enough,' Rabbit said. I agreed. Leaving 250 metres of open ground between us and the targets, we hit the ground.

'OK, Voodoo, Dusty, we're in position.'

'Roger that.'

A pause.

'Hang on to your nizzos, dudes. Frags coming over in three, two, one. . .'

We were too far away to see the projectiles being hurled over the front wall of the compound, but they clearly caught the attention of the targets. There was a sudden shout – something in Pashto, I couldn't tell what. The enemy started to run.

But too late.

A second later there were two orange flashes and, one after the other in quick succession, two loud cracks that echoed off the mountain slopes. I kept my eye on the kill zone. For a few seconds it was nothing but darkness and smoke. From the edge of my vision I saw the front gate to the compound open and two figures slip out. Voodoo and Dusty moved like lightning, firing suppressed bursts from their weapons into the confusion. I caught sight of another figure, just a silhouette, pushing himself up from the ground. A short burst from my rifle and he was back down again.

The contact couldn't have lasted more than twenty seconds, and now there was a sudden, eerie silence. Voodoo and Dusty started doubling towards us. We kept their positions covered. The fragmentation grenades had made enough noise to alert anyone to the fact that something was going down, so we needed to get to cover as quickly as possible.

The second Dusty and Voodoo were with us, we started retreating back to the firing point from which we'd taken out the snipers. We didn't get there a moment too soon. Just as we were scrambling behind the rubble, we saw two sets of headlamps pulling round into the area in front of the compound. I quickly checked them out through the Kite.

'OK, fellas,' I said. 'We got company.'

'How many?' Voodoo demanded. If he'd been fazed by the events of the last ninety minutes, he showed no sign of it. I was aware of the other three getting down into the firing position, ready for contact.

'Three open-top technicals. Five guys in each. Top-mounted machine-guns. Looks like they've got searchlights too, but they're not switched on.'

'Shit,' Rabbit said.

'Hold your fire,' I told them, and continued to examine the trucks. Two guys – they both wore shamags and had bandoliers of ammo strapped round their bodies – got out and examined the dead men on the ground. They said a few words to each other, then looked around. From their body language it looked like they didn't know where we were or which way we'd gone.

As I scoped the enemy, the others were talking in low, urgent tones. 'Where's Malouf?' Dusty demanded.

'We left him back at the wadi,' said Rabbit. 'He's got a beacon. If base want to come and get him, they know where he is.'

'He gave us another lead on Al-Zaranj's location,' I butted in.

Dusty snorted. 'Thing is, Jock, Malouf's track record ain't so good.'

'Let's just say I encouraged him to tell the truth this time round. There's a valley up in the mountain, locals call it Bakharov.' I still had my eye on the technicals. The two guys were climbing back into their vehicles. 'Whether he's shitting us or not, we have to check it out.'

I glanced at my watch: 03.00 hours. The sun would rise a few minutes after six.

'If Malouf's boss is in touch with Al-Zaranj, chances are our man knows we could be on to him. He'll want to move as soon as the sun comes up. That gives us a three-hour window.'

'We're going to need a bird,' said Dusty.

'I'm on it,' Voodoo replied. He shuffled back behind the firing position to radio back to base. Trouble was, Voodoo wasn't the only one to move. The three technicals were driving in our direction. They fanned out and came to a halt about twenty metres apart and a couple of hundred metres from our position. The enemy didn't know where we were, but there were only so many places we could hide. They'd made a guess and it was a good one.

Behind me, I could hear Voodoo calling in air support; but suddenly his voice was drowned by the sound of firing.

The machine-guns on the top of the three technicals opened up at exactly the same time. The two on the outside fired blindly into the desert, but the middle one was trained firmly on our firing position. The rounds splintered into the rubble, throwing up clouds of dust and showers of bullet-hard shrapnel.

Dusty, Rabbit and I rolled backwards.

'They're firing blind,' I hissed. 'They don't know we're here. If we return fire, we'll give away our position…'

Another burst of fire, followed by the faint noise of the technicals' engines coming close.

'Gimme some good news about that chopper, Voodoo,' Dusty growled. 'They're not morons out there. They know there are only a few places we can take cover. They'll flush us out sooner…'

A third burst of fire, higher this time so several rounds flew above our heads. I could feel the rush of air as they whizzed past.

'… or later.'

'Five minutes out,' Voodoo announced. 'We'll have to hold 'em back till then.'

As Voodoo spoke, the darkness was splintered by beams of light breaking over the rubble. At least one of the technicals had clearly switched on its searchlight, and it was aimed at our position. We could hear the enemy's voices now, shouting at each other from one vehicle to another.

'We can't let these fuckers get any closer,' Voodoo said. 'They'll be over us like rats.'

He was right. If we stayed where we were and they carried on advancing, we'd soon be surrounded. It would only be a matter of time before they saw us. Sometimes you've just got to take the fight to the enemy. We didn't have to win the battle; we just had to hold them back long enough for air support to get here.

'Roger that,' Dusty agreed. 'We got to take it to them.' I nodded, and so did Rabbit.

'Jock, Rabbit, take out the searchlights.' Made sense to put ourselves on a level playing field, rather than have us lit up like a fucking Christmas tree. 'Me and Dusty can go for the tyres. Once the machinery's down, we can start nailing the bad guys. Go for the machine-gunners first. We good with that?'

'I just hope that chopper gets here when it says it will,' I muttered.

'We just have to hold our position till it does.'

Another burst of fire thundered over our heads as each member of the patrol located a firing position. Rabbit and I took up the same positions we'd adopted when we were taking out the snipers, lying on our fronts over the top of the rubble, but slightly further apart this time – about five metres to stop ourselves bunching up and presenting an easy target. The other two got down to ground level – Voodoo to our left, Dusty to our right, peering round from the edges of the broken-down wall.

The searchlights were blinding. I didn't know if they lit me up or not, and I didn't bother to find out. I let loose a single round, which smashed straight into the face of the middle of the three searchlights. The machinery exploded.

'Go right,' I told Rabbit, before turning my aim towards the spotlight to my left. Less than a second later I'd taken it out, and Rabbit had done the same to his. But my eyes were dazzled and blinded, so I pulled myself back down below the line of fire until my vision returned.

I could hear Voodoo and Dusty laying down fire to my left and right, and amid the noise of gunfire came the tiny explosions of tyres being taken out. There was more shouting – I couldn't decipher it, but I could sure as hell tell they weren't talking about retreating. That was the trouble with these AQ fighters – half of them didn't care if they lived or died. It would have been madness for me to try to lay down rounds with my vision fucked, so I pulled two fragmentation grenades from my waistcoat, removed the pins and lobbed them towards the enemy.

'Frag out!' I shouted, then hunkered down, waiting for the explosions.

They came seconds later, and with them a terrible scream. One of the enemy had been hit by shrapnel and from the noises he was making, he wasn't long for this world. I blocked out the noise – not because it was distressing, but because it was distracting. I needed to keep my attention on the guys who could kill us, not the ones on the way out.

My vision restored, I got back into the firing position. I could see the wounded man about twenty metres in front of me. Half his face was gone and he was kneeling towards us. One of my patrol mates – I don't know who – put him out of his misery with a direct headshot that flung him back two metres in a frenzy of brain matter. The other targets had retreated from the area where the grenade had exploded, back towards their technicals. Each of the vehicles, though, still had a gunner at its mounted machine-gun. They had to be our next priority.

'Hit the gunners,' I told Rabbit. 'You go right, I'll go centre and left.'

Rabbit didn't reply. There was nothing to say. We just started laying down rounds together. My first burst took out the gunner of the middle technical. His body juddered to the back of the vehicle, but by that time I already had the vehicle to the left in my sights. Another burst and the second gunner was down.

We'd disabled the machine-guns but there was nothing to stop other members of the enemy crew from taking up position at the weapons, so we had to keep the firefight intense to discourage them from getting brave. Voodoo and Dusty each hurled out a grenade. A shout went up from the remaining enemy who, wherever they were, hit the deck seconds before the frags exploded. Rabbit and I didn't give them a chance to regroup: we just kept laying down rounds – short bursts, but frequent.

It was high-intensity and it kept the enemy at bay. But there was a limit to how long we could go on like this before we killed our ammo. 'Voodoo!' I shouted. 'We need that chopper!'

Bang on cue, I heard a noise in the distance behind us – like a fast-approaching wasp. I fired a final burst, catching a guy in the chest who was struggling towards the machine-guns. He was flung back in a shower of blood so hard that he disappeared over the back of the technical. I ducked back down below the firing line to reload my weapon when, lit up by the moon, I saw a cloud of dust in the desert. Two choppers were speeding towards us, one of them skirting low, only a few metres above the ground, the other above it and slightly to its fore. The lower chopper was an MI-8 – the same one that had set us down about five hours previously. The other was an MI-24 Hind, and that was extremely bad news for the AQ fighters who were trying to put holes in us at that very moment.

The Hind was an impressive beast even on the ground. In action, it was awesome. The pilot and co-pilot sat in tandem in tiered pods, one above the other. Two short wings sprouted from the side with rocket launchers fixed to the underside. At the front was a nose cannon that was controlled by the movement of the pilot's head. He just had to look where he wanted to fire, then press the button. When the Russians first brought these Hinds to Afghanistan, the only way the Mujahideen could down them was by getting up onto very high ground and firing on to the top of them. Eventually the Americans armed them with stinger missiles, but even then these choppers were hard to bring down – and had the capability to rain seven kinds of hell on to anyone who tried.

It was almost upon us when it rose higher into the air and hovered over our position, while the MI-8 held back about thirty metres, waiting for its attack helicopter chaperone to do its work. I was momentarily dazzled for a second time that night by the Hind's searchlights, so I couldn't see the pilot in his pod, moving his head to direct his weapon. I sure heard it, though – the characteristic chug-chugging of a nose gun as it showered rounds into the heart of the enemy. It fired continuously for thirty seconds, during which time Rabbit and I scrambled back down to ground level. I heard a massive explosion as one of the technicals' fuel tanks ignited. And when the nose cannon finally stopped firing – and the Hind spun in mid-air and hovered threateningly while the MI-8 came down to land on flat earth about twenty metres behind us – there was no sound of enemy weapons. We all knew what that meant.

The four of us doubled it back to the MI-8, heads low to protect ourselves from the downdraught, before flinging ourselves up the tailgate. The flight crew didn't fuck around. The tailgate was up and we were in the air within seconds and as I looked back over the village of Pajay I saw the lights of a third chopper descending on the southern edge near the wadi. It looked like they'd come in to scoop up Malouf. Give it a few minutes and he'd find himself on the wrong end of a Tier 1 field interrogation, but that was nothing to do with us now.

We had less than three hours till dawn, and we still had a job to do.

PSA
RT

XMIT

PSA
AUTO

LOCK

FUSE
ARM

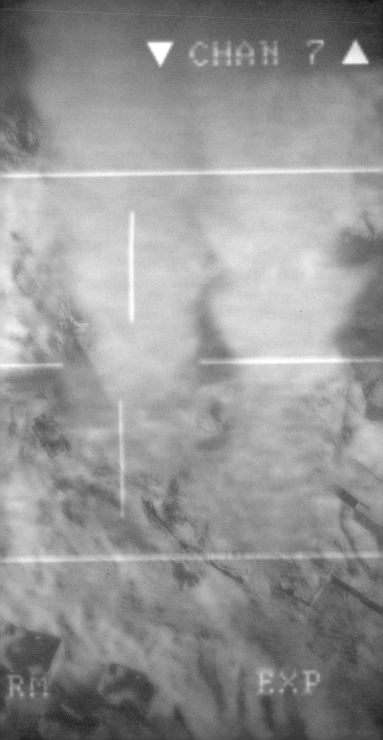

03.17 HRS.

Voodoo had clearly apprised base of the situation when he called in air support. We were barely off the ground when one of the flight crew handed us a map of the area. Pajay was marked in the centre. To the north, a mess of contour lines that indicated the sharp peaks of the mountain ranges. Someone had circled in pen an area approximately five klicks northwest of the village as the crow flew, where the markings clearly indicated a steep-sided valley. In clear capital letters was a single word: BAKHAROV.

The loadmaster approached us. 'We're setting you down two klicks to the east of the valley,' he shouted over the roar of the chopper's engines. 'We need to approach from the east so your target doesn't hear us flying over. There's a small plateau we can use as an LZ, but it's separated from the valley by a ridge about 300 metres high. You'll have to scale it before you can get into position.'

I glanced at the three others. Not even a flicker of concern. No sign that the contact from which we'd just been extracted had rattled them. Just looks of steely-eyed determination.

The loadie turned away from us for a moment, then returned with something in his hands. It was a rectangular box, about eight inches by five by two, and a small, sturdy tripod – a laser target designator. Nobody had to explain to us what that was for. Voodoo took hold of the LTD and stashed it in his Bergen, while I took delivery of a stash of mountain gear from the loadie. Then I gave myself a few moments to gather my thoughts. It had been a long night already, but it wasn't over yet.

From the side of the helicopter I could just see the tips of mountain ranges. The pilot was flying blind so there was no light from the aircraft, but the peaks had a silvery glow in the moonlight, broken up by the dark lines of deep ravines and hidden valleys. If Malouf was to be believed, somewhere down there, camouflaged by that forbidding landscape, was an important AQ operative called Al-Zaranj. He could hide wherever he wanted. But we were coming to get him.

Five minutes later the aircraft starting losing height. Voodoo, Dusty, Rabbit and I got our gear together and stood by the exit, ready to alight the moment we touched down. Blackness surrounded us as we lowered into the shadow of a deep valley, and there was a gentle bump as the helicopter hit the ground.

'*Go!*' shouted the loadie, and we were out. Seconds later the chopper was off. The pulsating sound of its rotor blades melted away, leaving us alone in the darkness and the silence.

We waited thirty seconds for our eyes to grow accustomed to the blackness and gradually our surroundings became clearer. The flat area where we had landed was small – about twenty metres square. On two sides were steep slopes, which disappeared up into the darkness, beyond which the amazing canopy of the night sky gleamed brightly.

I was aware of movement from Voodoo. He was unfolding the map the loadmaster had given us and removing a torch from his pack. The torch had a thin, highly directional beam to stop any light spill from illuminating our position, and it had been fitted with a red filter so that white light wouldn't wreck our night eyes. It took Voodoo less than a minute to get his bearings. He pointed up one of the slopes. 'North,' he said curtly. 'Let's get climbing.'

It was a steep slope, which made the going hard, especially with the weight of our equipment, and the ground underneath was covered with loose rocks, which meant we had to tread carefully in the darkness. We'd been ascending for about thirty minutes, when the terrain changed and a sheer rock face loomed up in front of us. Difficult in the dark to tell how high it was. Thirty-five metres. Maybe forty. We scouted left and right, trying to see if there was any other way up. Nothing. We were going to have to scale the cliff.

'OK, fellas,' I told the others. 'I'll lead.'

Mountaineering was my bag. I'd spent a year in Germany on the Alpine Guides Course, and while the arid mountains of Afghanistan were different to the peaks of the Alps, the principles were the same.

I removed my Bergen and started going through the mountaineering gear I'd taken from the loadie: a stash of friends – essential pieces of equipment that could be wedged into cracks in the wall so that I could get a line up – and a forty-metre fixed line; a roll of webbing tape; everything I needed to get a line up to the top of the cliff face so the others could follow. I put the end of the line round Rabbit's waist, who had a carabina attached to his belt loop, then slung the rest of it round my waist and engaged my NV goggles. 'See you at the top, guys,' I said.

I moved as quickly as possible, hunting out cracks in the wall where I could wedge in my friends before threading the line through them. It took twenty-five minutes to reach the top and throw down a second line so that I could haul the Bergens and other equipment up before Voodoo, Dusty and Rabbit made their ascents. They climbed quickly, using with ease the line I'd set up. They were up in less than fifteen minutes – an impressive feat, though I guess I shouldn't have been surprised.

But there wasn't time for backslapping. Time check: 04.37. Less than two hours till sunrise. We had to press on.

We continued scrambling upwards. Sweat was pouring from my body even though our altitude was increasing and it was not yet daylight. My muscles burned, but I just focused on the job ahead. We reached the top of the ridge at 05.02. There was no time to stop. Voodoo studied his map, lying low so nobody could see the tiny amount of light coming from his torch. He pointed down into the valley below us. 'That's Bakharov.'

'Let's get closer,' I said, 'then find ourselves a lying-up position. Sunrise in about an hour. We haven't got much time. And guys, go soft. Al-Zaranj might have spotters out. Let's not warn them we're on their case, huh?'

We scrambled down the slope – slowly and carefully so we didn't alert anyone with our noise, or with loose rocks tumbling down into the valley. We covered about 600 metres in twenty minutes, and by this time we could see the base of the valley with the naked eye. It was 200 metres away and snaked north to south.

Voodoo raised a hand and we all stopped. Thirty metres off to the left there were two jagged boulders – each of them five metres wide and a couple high – that appeared to be leaning against each other. There was a triangular gap between the two, half a metre in width at its base and a metre high, angled slightly so it faced northeast along the valley. A bunch of other boulders were dotted around at irregular intervals too, so these two larger ones didn't stick out too badly. The hiding place they created was the biggest we could see – not ideal, but it would serve as an OP, so we made for it.

Voodoo, Dusty and Rabbit took up position behind the boulders, checking their weapons and prepping the LTD, while I scoped out the valley. The grainy-green picture was hard to decipher because there wasn't much ambient light in the valley for the Kite to magnify.

'What you getting, Jock?'

I scoped for another twenty seconds before replying. 'No sign of habitation,' I reported. 'Malouf said there was a cave system. I can't make anything out, but the far side of the valley's in deep shadow. We'll have to mark time till dawn.'

'Roger that.'

Waiting can be a dangerous game. It's easy for your attention to wander, your readiness to drop. There was none of that those last few minutes before dawn. I continued to scope with my night sight; the others were armed and ready. We all kept absolutely still. If no one knew we were here, it was unlikely that we'd be seen; but the second they detected movement, we'd be compromised.

It was around 05.40 that I started to detect a slightly different quality to the darkness as dawn approached. The Kite detected it too as gradually the details on the far side of the valley floor opened up. It was arid and boulder-strewn and I could just make out deep rivulets in the floor. Water clearly ran through here in the winter, but now, at the dog end of summer, it was desert-dry. And on the far side of the valley floor, 250 metres from our position, I saw it. The cave mouth was only a small opening, some two metres wide and three high. And just as I'd clocked it, I picked up movement. A figure emerged into the valley.

'I've got someone,' I breathed.

'Take your time, Jock. Let's have a positive ID before we start making decisions.'

He was right. Nobody wanted to start getting heavy with a bunch of innocent Afghan hermits. Just because a guy had walked out of a cave, it didn't make him an AQ target. I examined him through the Kite. He was wearing robes and had a shamag wrapped round his head, which obscured his features. No weapon that I could see.

The figure stopped outside the cave and looked round. The guys were totally still as I watched him for a good minute. Silence all around. Like hunters stalking their prey.

The guy moved. His hands went up to his shamag and he started to peel it off from round his head. I zoomed in on him, so that his face filled the field of my Kite, and I had to steady my hand to stop that hazy green image from juddering now that I was focused so far in. He unwound the shamag three times before revealing his face.

He looked young. Only a hint of a beard.

'Negative ID,' I breathed. 'It's not Al-Zaranj, fellas.'

Dusty, Voodoo and Rabbit didn't reply. They didn't even move. They knew that right now patience was their best friend, and I could sense that they, like me, were wound up like tightly coiled springs.

I zoomed out. The guy looked around again, then slung his shamag over his shoulder and walked back into the cave.

I lowered the scope and looked up. The inky sky had become steely, and the stars were receding. No sign yet of the sun, but dawn was upon us. Keeping my movements to a minimum, I stashed the Kite and replaced it with an ordinary day-vision scope, before settling down to watch again.

We didn't have to wait long for more movement. Five minutes, perhaps, before five men walked out. This time they were armed. Three of them had what looked like regular AK-47s slung across their backs, but two others carried the Krinkov variant with its short barrel.

It was one of these that I recognized.

I'd only seen one picture of Al-Zaranj, back at the FOB the previous evening. But one was enough.

We'd all been trained to take mental snapshots. And there was no doubt about it. Al-Zaranj, our high-value AQ target, was there. He was talking to the other man with the Krink and they were pointing along the floor of the valley. It was impossible to hear what they were saying, of course, but they looked like they were discussing their departure.

'We've got him,' I whispered.

There were no sudden movements. Shielded by the boulder, Rabbit set up the LTD on its sturdy little tripod, directing it towards the cave through the triangular space between the boulders, while Voodoo got on the radio to base. 'Zero, this is Voodoo. We have positive ID. Repeat, we have positive ID.'

I maintained eyes on the target. Al-Zaranj disappeared back into the cave, leaving the remaining four outside. Thirty seconds later three more men appeared. They were carrying crates, which they set down outside the cave mouth. I couldn't tell for sure what was in them, but I reckoned it was ammo.

Voodoo updated us. 'They're sending in Hellfires. Rabbit, laze the target. We've got ourselves a UAV in the vicinity.'

'Roger that,' Rabbit replied.

It would be a clinical strike. The UAV, controlled from thousands of miles away at MacDill, would be circling high in the sky, out of sight. Once we'd lazed the position of the cave, the UAV would be able to dispatch Hellfires, which would pick up the laser signal and be guided on to the cave with pinpoint accuracy. At least that was the idea. We all knew how great the potential was for a fuck-up.

If the coordinates transmitted were wrong by just a whisper, the Hellfires could be taking *us* out, not Al-Zaranj. No one wanted a blue on blue, and I could sense the tension in the unit.

'Take your time, Rabbit,' Dusty murmured. 'This ain't a good moment for mistakes.'

Rabbit barely acknowledged him. His mind was clearly on doing the job right, not on worrying what might happen if he got it wrong. There was a whirring sound as the LTD warmed up. Rabbit looked through the viewfinder. 'Lazing target now,' he reported quietly.

The LTD continued to whirr.

Voodoo said later that we should have predicted what happened next. It was typical of him. Never satisfied. Always learning. I'd heard him say before that Tier 1 selection was an ongoing project. I guess that's what he meant. And maybe he was right. Maybe we should have predicted that at some stage the sun would appear over the low peaks at the end of the valley.

A sudden, piercing shard of light lit up our position. We might have got away with it, had the sunlight not reflected off the lens of the LTD.

The enemy saw it immediately – a glint up on the side of the valley that gave away our position. One of Al-Zaranj's men – the young guy who I'd seen unwrap the shamag from round his head – pointed directly at us, and suddenly there was the sound of shouting.

'*We're spotted!*' I yelled. No need for secrecy now. '*Fucking heads down!*'

Half the enemy disappeared into the cave. The remainder started aiming their weapons in our direction. I quickly hurled myself behind the protection of the boulders as a round hit the stony ground just around us, causing a little explosion of dust and a ricochet of pebble fragments.

'Rabbit, you good to go?'

'Negative.' He kept his eyes at the LTD, fully in the view of the enemy, but no less collected for that. 'Hold 'em back,' he instructed. 'I need another thirty seconds.'

'You got it, buddy,' Voodoo replied. Another enemy round splintered into the front of the boulders, followed by a sudden burst from the valley floor. Voodoo swung round from the side of the boulder and aimed his rifle towards the valley floor. A quick burst of fire and he found cover again.

More shouting down below. Urgent. Confused. I put myself in the line of fire to send another burst of rounds down towards the enemy, and I saw one guy on the ground. The others ignored him. They were yelling at each other, running around chaotically. Someone ran out from inside the cave. He carried a rocket launcher on his shoulder, and even from this distance I could see he had one up the spout.

'*RPG!*' I shouted, and pulled back behind the boulder just as we heard the whooshing sound of the grenade speeding in our direction. All four of us hit the ground, including Rabbit, but the LTD stayed intact on its tripod, beaming its laser towards the target. I covered my head with my arms, just in time to hear the RPG starbursting a couple of metres short of our position. The shrapnel rained against the front of the boulders, falling harmlessly. But we knew that the next time they shot a grenade in our direction, we might not be so lucky.

'Dusty!' Voodoo shouted. 'Get that fucker with the launcher!'

'Let's boogie,' said Dusty.

Of all of us, he was the sharpest shooter. I'd heard that back home Dusty was a hunter and had been honing his skills since he was a kid. He pulled himself up and got down on one knee in the space between the two boulders that Rabbit had just vacated. Dusty didn't need more than a second to take aim. Just a single shot. I heard a man scream down below.

'*Rabbit, did you get it?*' Voodoo yelled.

'I got it.'

'Zero, this is Voodoo. The target is marked. Repeat, the target is marked.'

'*RPG!*' It was Dusty who shouted it this time. Whether someone had reloaded the dead shooter's launcher or emerged from the cave with a second one, I couldn't tell. All I heard was the dreaded noise of the grenade fizzing towards us – over our heads this time – before it slammed into the hillside behind us. Another shower of shrapnel. Close this time. The enemy were getting their eye in.

I crawled back round the corner of the boulder and quickly took in what was happening. Two of the men were advancing towards us, about 100 metres away. The rest were retreating back into the cave. I couldn't figure out what they were doing, but the advancing ones had to be stopped. I took out the guy on my side with a burst that ripped into the top of his chest. At the same time, Dusty got his mate with a headshot, and the two bodies tumbled a couple of metres down the hillside. By now, though, more guys were emerging from the cave, and they had something with them.

'Dushka!' Dusty screamed, and he was bang on. The Russian DShK machine-gun was already on its mount and being manhandled out of the cave by two men. Four others started raining covering fire on us, so Dusty and I were forced to take cover behind the boulders.

'It's gonna get noisy!'

It was Dusty again, but Voodoo barely acknowledged him. He glanced at his watch and then looked up to the sky. I followed his gaze.

I knew what Voodoo was looking for, but there was nothing. Just the clear blue of early morning. We could only hope that the LTD was transmitting its coordinates to the UAV that was supposed to be circling thousands of metres in the air.

Suddenly the air was filled with the sound of thunder as the enemy pumped the Russian equivalent of .50-cal rounds towards our position. At first the incoming fire flew over the boulders and slammed into the hillside, but as the gunner adjusted his aim, the rounds started slamming into the front of them.

'Watch the LTD!' Voodoo shouted. 'That thing gets hit, we're fucked…'

Just as he spoke, a burst of rounds flew through the triangular gap, inches above the laser target designator. The tripod wobbled slightly from the air displacement, but it then steadied itself. We were pinned down, unable to move as the brutal rounds from that machine-gun ripped through the air.

A sudden silence.

'*Go!*' Voodoo hissed.

All four of us moved quickly, putting ourselves out in the open and laying down rounds while the enemy changed the machine-gun link. None of us needed to tell the others to keep away from the LTD. We needed to draw their fire away from it, so we positioned ourselves on either side of the lying-up position.

Two more men went down, but we didn't have more than ten seconds to fire before the DShK was up and running again and we had to press ourselves back behind the boulders. The air filled once more with the din of machine-gun rounds.

Rabbit's face was dripping sweat. He moistened his lips with his tongue. '*The more they fire,*' he shouted, '*the less ammo they have. They can't keep this up forever. When the DShK's out, they're ours.*'

Voodoo was on his knees looking up into the sky again, like a man praying. Not that any of us were the praying type. '*Won't be necessary!*' he shouted, and there was a ghost of a smile on his face as he pointed upwards.

They looked very tiny at first. Just two dots in the sky that could have been mistaken for anything – a couple of birds, maybe, or very distant aircraft. But they quickly grew bigger, zeroing in on our position with brutal, pinpoint accuracy.

'*Hit the ground!*' Voodoo shouted, but he needn't have. We knew what those dots in the sky were, and what kind of effect they were going to have.

The Hellfires took another ten seconds to reach us. They weren't noisy as they flew into the valley, but even if they had been – we wouldn't have been able to hear them over the noise of the DShK that was still hurling rounds at our position.

We certainly heard the moment they hit, though. The sudden explosions were short – one after the other, with only a microsecond between them – but the booms echoed deafeningly off the valley walls as the heat from the blast scorched the air around us and the shockwaves knocked the LTD off its tripod. The moment the earth stopped shaking, I pulled myself out from the LUP, keeping low to the ground as we crawled round to view the damage. Huge clouds of smoke were billowing out from the cave, and I could hear the sound of ammo exploding inside. Above the cave mouth I could just make out hunks of rock tumbling to the ground. I kept my rifle at the ready, prepared to shoot anyone I saw escaping from the blast site.

But there was no one. A direct strike from two Hellfire missiles. Nobody was going to survive that.

From behind me, I heard Voodoo on the radio. 'Zero, this is Voodoo. The enemy have gone to bed. Repeat, the enemy have gone to bed.'

I allowed myself a smile for the first time in twelve hours. 'Understatement of the year,' I muttered to myself. 'Understatement of the fucking year.'

06.30 HRS.

It took several minutes for the smoke to clear. We didn't let our concentration drop. Just because the guys inside Al-Zaranj's cave were bargaining their way into paradise didn't mean the Hellfire strike would not have been heard for miles around, and there was no guarantee we wouldn't start drawing fire from other AQ targets that might be in the vicinity. So, while Voodoo called in a chopper to extract us, and Rabbit packed up the LTD, Dusty and I scoped the surrounding area, alert to movement or anything suspicious.

Nothing doing. The valley was as dead as Al-Zaranj himself and within ten minutes we heard the unmistakable sound of a chopper approaching. The MI-8 came over the brow of the valley, accompanied by its Hind chaperone, which now swooped in towards the ground and hovered just above the cave mouth, its nose gun moving left and right with the pilot's head, ready to counter-attack any nasty surprises while the MI-8 came in to land. We scrambled down the stony hillside to where the chopper was setting down, bowing low on account of the downdraught. Twenty metres from the MI-8's position, I passed the remnants of a severed limb, bloody and gore-spattered. It wouldn't be there long – no doubt a wild animal would be glad of it before the following night was over.

The chopper rose up the moment we were all in. Within seconds we were above the ridgeline, the Hind offering us rear support, looking down on the scene of devastation below. And soon we were high enough to see the whole mountain range, purple and grey in the early morning sun, and the village of Pajay beyond. Beautiful place Afghanistan, looked at from up here. Shame it was such a shithole on the ground. And none of us were under any illusions that it was going to get better any time soon.

The FOB was just the same as it had been the previous morning. Busy. Hot. As we set down, left the aircraft and started trudging towards the tents, nobody came up to ask us what had been going down that night. Everyone else had their own jobs to think about and we weren't about to go singing about our exploits. All in a night's work. Eventful, certainly, but it wasn't the first – and it sure as hell wouldn't be the last. Especially not for Voodoo, Dusty and Rabbit. I might have an all-expenses-paid trip back to Hereford that day. For them, the battle was ongoing. It was no secret that the Americans had big plans for The Stan, and with operators like Dusty, Voodoo and Rabbit in country, the next few weeks and months would be a bad time to be in the Taliban.

Back in the tent, we got liquid inside us like it was going out of fashion. We didn't discuss what had happened that night. What was there *to* discuss? Job done. Move on. Members from other teams who'd been out on the ground drifted in. I found myself in the company of my SAS mates; Voodoo and Rabbit were in another part of the tent talking to their Neptune colleagues; Dusty was surrounded by Wolfpack.

It was a couple of hours before I managed to get a bit of time to myself. I was sitting on my Bergen in the corner of the tent with a bottle of tepid water when Dusty approached me with something in his hands. He threw it in my direction and I caught it.

'What's this?'

'American MRE, dude. Can't bear to watch you eating any more of that British shit.' He looked over his shoulder. 'You chose the wrong time to be bugging out on us, my friend. Voodoo and Rabbit just got the word to move into Gardez. Some dude there called Tariq wants to tell us where the AQ forces are amassing.'

'Hope he's more reliable than Malouf.'

Dusty shrugged. 'They'll deal with it. Either way, things are about to get spicy.'

I looked across the tent. Voodoo and Rabbit were by the entrance. Voodoo nodded at me. It wasn't much. No great show of emotion, but I got the gesture. We'd fought alongside each other. It made us brothers. We understood. Rabbit was flipping his lucky rabbit-foot talisman in his hand. He inclined his head in my direction. Both of them looked exhausted, but I knew that wasn't going to stop them from doing what needed to be done. Guys like that, they thrive on the adrenaline. Guys like *us*. I realised with a pang that deep down I didn't much want to be leaving theatre. Still, it wasn't like it was forever.

'I get the feeling I'll be back in country pretty soon…' I told Dusty.

He gave me a look as if to say, 'Whatever', then put his dark glasses back on and turned his back on me. 'Enjoy your breakfast, my friend,' he called as he walked away.

I looked at the foil package in my hands, then ripped open the top, suddenly realizing how damn hungry I was. I found a spoon from my pack and started shovelling the food into my mouth. It wasn't so bad, but truth to tell, it wasn't so much different to the British stuff. Same shit, I reckoned, different package.

A bit like the four of us who'd been on patrol that night, I thought to myself as I continued to eat. Different accents. Different training. But same attitude. Same single-minded determination. Same resolve to get the job done. In a world where reputation was everything, I reckoned ours were still intact.

Yeah. Same shit, different package. I continued to eat Dusty's MRE, and waited for my transport home.

THIS IS THE FACE
THE ENEMY FEARS

THIS IS FORCE MULTIPLIED.
RELENTLESS. EXACTING. PRECISE.

THIS IS A NEW BREED OF WARRIOR.
FOR A NEW BREED OF WARFARE.

THIS IS TIER 1.

DOMINATE
E MULTIPLAYER

JOIN THE ELITE AS
A TIER 1 OPERATOR

MEDAL OF
HONOR
MEDALOFHONOR.COM

 XBOX 360 XBOX LIVE PC DVD PS3 DICE EA 15.10.10

ALSO AVAILABLE BY CHRIS RYAN

The guys in the Regiment know they face their fiercest enemies when they fight the Taliban. No-one is tougher, more deadly – or more cunning. And if they enter the Taliban's kill zone, they know just what to expect…

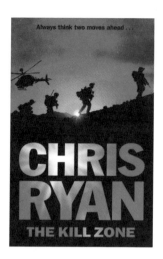

When three deadly Stinger missiles go missing in Helmand Province, the Regiment is tasked to retrieve the weapons at all costs. SAS legend Jack Harker has to lead an eight-man mission into a suspected Taliban facility. He's suspicious about what the aims of the mission really are – and it's about to go noisy.

Meanwhile, in Belfast, Siobhan Byrne, a highly trained surveillance operative, is infiltrating the drug crew of a former IRA commander. But are her motives professional or personal? Even she doesn't know any more.

Neither Jack nor Siobhan can guess just how closely linked their operations are about to become, or just what's at stake. But as the President of the United States makes plans to visit the UK, a devastating plot unfolds.

The Kill Zone is available now from **www.amazon.co.uk**   CORONET